Judith Koppens & Anouk Nijs

Mila

Wants to Go to School

Clavis

NEW YORK

I'm Mila.
Sometimes I live with
my daddy and sometimes
I live with my mommy.
Today I am with Daddy,
and I'm excited because it's my first day of school.
Daddy is going to take me there.

I've finished my breakfast and packed
Cuddle Monkey in my backpack.
I am ready to go to school.
"Hurry, Daddy – finish your breakfast.
I want to go."
"Coming," mumbles Daddy.

"But first I have to put on my shoes," Daddy says. "And let me put Pepper on his leash."

I am already at the door.
Why is Daddy taking so long?
I don't want to be late for school.

Mrs. Rose is outside getting her mail.
Daddy stops to say hello.

Whew!
It's taking forever.
Daddy, hurry up!

"Look, Mila," Daddy says.
"The deer are in the meadow.
Should we go and take a look?"

"No, Daddy! I want to get to school!"

"Well, how about
the playground, Mila?"
Daddy asks. "Do you want
to stop and go on the swing?"

"No, Daddy!
I don't want to go on the swing.
I want to go to school!" Daddy is
being a real dilly-dally.
I'm going to be late!

Finally we get to school.
My teacher is waiting outside.
She waves to me and I wave back.

"Hi, Mila – it's so nice to have you here,"
Ms. O'Connor says. "Come inside and I'll
show you where you can hang your jacket."

Daddy walks me to my classroom. And then it's time to say goodbye. Daddy looks sad. "Are you sure you don't want to come home with me?" he asks. "I'm going to miss you while you're in school."

"Silly Dad – if I go home with you, I'll miss all the fun things at school. I am going to draw and sing songs, eat a snack, and play outside."

I give Daddy a big hug.
"I'll see you after school when you pick me up. I'm going to play with my new friends, but you will always be my Daddy!"

"Bye, sweet Mila. Have fun today!"
"Bye, Daddy. I will see you again soon!"